Hedgehog Needs a Hug

JEN BETTON

G. P. PUTNAM'S SONS

For Mark,

who gives the best hugs.

G. P. PUTNAM'S SONS
an imprint of Penguin Random House LLC
375 Hudson Street
New York, NY 10014

G. P. Putnam's Sons is a registered trademark of Penguin Random House LLC.

Library of Congress Cataloging-in-Publication Data
Names: Betton, Jen, author, illustrator.
Title: Hedgehog needs a hug / Jen Betton.
Description: New York, NY : G. P. Putnam's Sons, [2018]
Summary: Hedgehog wakes up needing a hug, but has trouble finding a friend who will get so close to his prickles.
Identifiers: LCCN 2016044473 | ISBN 9781524737122 (hardcover)
Subjects: | CYAC: Hedgehogs—Fiction. | Hugging—Fiction. | Forest animals—Fiction.
Classification: LCC PZ7.1.B49 Hed 2018 | DDC [Fic]—dc23
LC record available at https://lccn.loc.gov/2016044473

Manufactured in China by RR Donnelley Asia Printing Solutions Ltd.
ISBN 9781524737122
1 3 5 7 9 10 8 6 4 2

Design by Jaclyn Reyes.
Text set in Plantagenet Cherokee Regular.
The illustrations were done in watercolor, pastel, and colored pencil, with digital adjustments.

When Hedgehog awoke in his cozy nest, he felt down in the snout and droopy in the prickles. *I'll feel better if I get a hug,* he thought.

Hedgehog poked his nose
into the sunshine and toddled
toward Rabbit's grassy den.

"Rabbit, I need a hug. Will you
give me one?" he asked.

"I'm sorry, Hedgehog." Rabbit slowly backed away. "Um, I have the sniffles. I'm afraid I will give you a cold if I hug you," she said.

And hippity-skippity-scram, she was
gone. "Aaaachoo!" echoed out of the den.
Poor rabbit, thought Hedgehog.

Hedgehog wandered across
the clearing to the hollow log
where Raccoon slept.

"Raccoon, I need a hug. Will
you give me one?" he asked.

"I'm sorry, Hedgehog." Raccoon ducked back into the shadows. "Uh, I'm afraid I have the most frightful garbage breath—you don't want to come near me!" he exclaimed.

And he scuffle-scoot-scampered into the dark of his log.

"I don't mind garbage breath," called Hedgehog, but Raccoon was gone.

Hedgehog trudged over to Turtle's
sun-soaked resting spot. "Turtle?"

Zzzzzz

"Never mind." Hedgehog
sighed, and he shuffled away.

Hedgehog didn't see anyone else to ask.
Was there no one who would hug him?

"I'm so sorry no one will give you a hug,"
drawled Fox, sly-slide-slinking over. "I'm not afraid
of your spines, little Hedgehog . . .

"I'll even give you a big KISS!"

Hedgehog scurried into the bracken.

He shuddered, thinking of Fox's sharp teeth.

He was very tired of asking for hugs.

Maybe he should just go home.

Then Hedgehog heard soft sobs coming
from the clearing beyond his bush.
"What's the matter, Skunk?" Hedgehog
asked, keeping his distance.

"No one will give me a hug,
and I feel so blue," Skunk said.

Hedgehog took a deep breath and tip-patter-padded close to Skunk. "I feel blue, too, Skunk. I will give you a hug."

Skunk looked at Hedgehog's prickles . . .
then she slowly opened her arms.

Very gently, Hedgehog gave her a hug.

And they both felt better.